CAPTAIN ZAP

AND THE EVIL BARON VON FISHHEAD

by Jon Buller and Susan Schade

A Step 3 Book

Random House 🏠 New York

"KA-BOOM! KA-BOOM! KA-BOOM!"

My friend Cosmo and I like making up comics. We take turns drawing.

Cosmo's character is THE EVIL BARON VON FISHHEAD, who wants to rule all the beaches in the world.

Cosmo had just drawn Fishhead blowing up a whole row of lifeguard stands.

Then it was my turn.

My character is CAPTAIN ZAP, the Electric Man. He is sworn to protect life and personal property and is Fishhead's archenemy.

"I'll get you for this, Fishhead, you fiend," I said in my best Captain Zap voice. "As soon as I discover the location of your secret UNDERWATER LABORATORY!"

"MWA-HA-HA!" Cosmo laughed
Fishhead's evil laugh as he drew Fishhead
diving into the ocean.

"Luckily, Captain Zap can't swim!"
Cosmo wrote in the speech balloon.

I had to laugh at Cosmo's drawing. "Did
you ever notice how much Fishhead looks
like my goldfish Bernice?" I said.

"He does? Let's see." Cosmo jumped up
to look in my fish tank.

"Hey, Perry!" he cried. "I think one of
your fish is dead!"

He was right. One of the goldfish in
my aquarium was floating on the surface,
belly up.

"Poor Rupert," I said sadly.

"Let's bury him," Cosmo said.

I found a little box. Cosmo scooped Rupert out of the water and put him in the box.

We took the box out to the backyard. I picked a spot and started digging.

Clink! I hit a rock or something. I dug the shovel in again. *Clink!*

"That doesn't sound like a stone," Cosmo
said. "I'll bet it's buried treasure! Here!" He
grabbed the shovel. "Let *me* do it."

He made a big deal out of loosening the dirt. Finally, he pushed the shovel in deep and pried out a long metal box.

"Don't open it!" I said, holding my nose.
"It's that snake we buried last month! I'll
bet it *really* stinks now!"

"We didn't bury the snake in a box,"
Cosmo said. "We used a paper bag,
remember?"

"Oh, yeah," I said.

Cosmo opened the box.

There was nothing inside except two pencils.

"That's weird," I said. "Why would anybody bury two pencils in a box?"

Cosmo shrugged. He kept one pencil and gave the other one to me. I put it in my pocket.

We laid Rupert's box in the hole and covered it with dirt.

We had a moment of silence in his memory. Then Cosmo went home.

Later that night, Cosmo called me up.

"I have an idea for a Captain Zap comic," he said. "Suppose Fishhead sneaks into Captain Zap's house and leaves a magic shrinking potion someplace where Captain Zap will drink it?"

I pulled a pencil out of my pocket and started drawing a bottle.

"Yeah," I said. "And he disguises it as Captain Zap's favorite soda!" I wrote *Fizzo* on the bottle.

Just as I finished the word *Fizzo*—
POP!—there was a little explosion on my
paper, and a *real* bottle appeared on my
desk! The paper, where I had just drawn
the soda bottle, was now blank!

"Whoa!" I gasped.

Cosmo said, "Did you say something?"

I looked in amazement at the bottle.
Then at my paper. Then at my pencil.

It was one of the pencils that had been
buried in the ground. As I looked at it, it
started to glow and sizzle in my hand. I
dropped it like a hot potato!

"Hey, Perry, are you still there?"

I needed to think. I said, "Cosmo, you know those pencils we found today? Don't draw anything with yours."

"Why not?" Cosmo asked.

"Bring it over tomorrow and I'll explain," I said. "I gotta go." I hung up before he could argue.

I picked up the pencil again. It still felt warm. Was it magic?

I thought for a minute. Then I began drawing a picture of a model train locomotive that I really, really wanted.

POP!

There it was. Right on my desk. A real, live model train engine. Cool!

I picked it up. It was awesome! And it had lots more detail than my drawing. In fact, it looked *exactly* like a real train engine!

And then it hit me. *What if it* had *been a real train?! Full-size instead of miniature? It would have wrecked the house!!*

I hid the pencil in a safe place. Then I opened the bottle of shrinking potion. I was dying to try it, but I'm too smart for that. I poured it down the sink instead.

I had a hard time getting to sleep that night.

The next day an incredible machine roared up in front of my house.

I ran out to look.

The passenger door opened and out stepped—*Cosmo!*

He put his hand on the hood of the car and said, "How do you like her?"

That's when I realized what had
happened. Cosmo had *drawn* the car
with his magic pencil!

The driver revved the engine a few
times, then roared down the street.

I grabbed Cosmo's arm. "I thought I
told you not to use the pencil!" I hissed.

"So what!" He jerked his arm away. "I'll bet you did!"

"Well, yeah." I showed him my model train engine.

"How come it came out so small?" Cosmo asked.

"Because I'm smarter than you are. I *drew* a model, and the pencil *made* a model. What happened when you drew the car, anyway? Did it bust down a wall?"

"Nah. The car showed up outside in the driveway. The driver, too."

"Wow," I said. "These pencils are really smart!"

We went out back and knelt down with our pads of paper and our magic pencils.

"Okay," I said, "what should we draw first?"

Cosmo didn't answer. He was
already drawing. He was making this
evil face that he always makes when
he draws Fishhead.

"Hey!" I said. "Wait! Don't—"

But it was too late.

POP! Fishhead burst off the paper
and swooped up into the sky.

"MWA-HA-HA!" he laughed. And
Cosmo was gone!

I couldn't believe what was happening! Cosmo hadn't just created Fishhead, he had turned into him! I had always told him he identified too much with Fishhead.

Well, there was only one man who was a match for the evil Baron von Fishhead. I started drawing, and the pencil did the rest.

BOING! My head was ringing. I felt powerful. I flew into the air and soared over the town with my pad and pencil.

ZAP! I let loose an electric energy bolt on a rock below, just to try it out. The rock sizzled into a smoking pile of ash. Whoa!

I had *become* CAPTAIN ZAP!

I looked around for Fishhead.

I found him—flying over the beach, drawing on his pad and laughing like a maniac.

What evil scheme was he cooking up now?

Then I saw the ocean below begin to
bubble and swell.

A giant green claw reached out of the
water, followed by two huge eyes! A crab
the size of a house burst out of the sea
and scuttled up the beach.

I realized at once that Fishhead must
have drawn it. There wasn't a moment
to lose!

Captain Zap never zaps living creatures, so I drew a Shrink-O-Ray, grabbed it in midair, and flew after the giant crab.

"Take that! And that!" I blasted it twice, and the crab shrank and retreated under a rock.

It was a victory for Captain Zap. But Fishhead was still on the loose.

"Help! Help!" I heard someone scream.
Uh-oh. I looked around.

A huge squid was wrapping its tentacles
around a sailboat. Two frightened people
were clinging to the mast and screaming
for help.

Quickly I drew a rescue helicopter with a rope ladder hanging off it. And just as the squid crushed the boat to smithereens, the boaters grabbed the rope ladder and were saved! A blast from the Shrink-O-Ray took care of the giant squid.

Now, if only I could find a way to stop Fishhead before his giant sea creatures took over the beach!

With Captain Zap's binocular x-ray vision, I scanned the shore.

I finally spotted Fishhead behind a fishing shack. He was drawing furiously and snickering to himself.

POP!

A strange device appeared on the roof of the shack. I recognized it right away. It was one of Fishhead's remote-control seaweed launchers—and it was pointing at *me!*

WHOOSH! It launched a big glob of
seaweed.

FWOP! Before I had time to dodge it,
I was all tangled up in slimy seaweed.
I couldn't see! I couldn't fly! I was falling
down to the sea!

But Captain Zap is not so easily captured! I sent an atomic-energy bolt through my entire body. *ZAP!* The seaweed was cooked to a crisp and I was free!

This time, Fishhead had gone too far.
He had to be stopped!

I drew a jet-propelled pencil sharpener,
and I sent it after Fishhead's pencil.

Fishhead dove into the water, trying to escape from the flying pencil sharpener.

At the same time, he must have copied my idea and sent his own pencil sharpener after me. But he had made *his* invisible!

Before I knew what was happening,
I felt my pencil being pulled right out
of my hand. I saw it reduced to sawdust.
And then I began falling to the ground.

I landed with a THUD right in my own
backyard. I checked myself for broken
bones and struggled to my feet. I felt
wobbly and heavy, as if I were made out
of lead.

I had lost my Captain Zap powers.

I was just me again.

THWAP! Cosmo landed on the ground beside me, dripping wet. He looked stunned.

I wasn't sure I wanted him for a friend anymore. "Hey!" I said. "You tried to drown me!"

"It wasn't me!" Cosmo cried. "It was Fishhead! He took over. I couldn't stop him!"

"Yeah, those pencils *were* pretty dangerous," I said. "I guess that's why somebody buried them. But you shouldn't have drawn Fishhead in the first place."

"I know. I'm sorry," Cosmo said.

We shook hands. We were friends again.

"You know what I was thinking?" Cosmo asked as we went inside. "This would make a great comic!"

He was right!